DEBBIE WHITE

Illustrated by Chris Smedley

OXFORD
UNIVERSITY PRESS

OXFORD

UNIVERSITY PRESS

Great Clarendon Street, Oxford OX2 6DP

Oxford University Press is a department of the University of Oxford.
It furthers the University's objective of excellence in research, scholarship,
and education by publishing worldwide in

Oxford   New York

Auckland   Cape Town   Dar es Salaam   Hong Kong   Karachi
Kuala Lumpur   Madrid   Melbourne   Mexico City   Nairobi
New Delhi   Shanghai   Taipei   Toronto

With offices in

Argentina   Austria   Brazil   Chile   Czech Republic   France   Greece
Guatemala   Hungary   Italy   Japan   Poland   Portugal   Singapore
South Korea   Switzerland   Thailand   Turkey   Ukraine   Vietnam

Oxford is a registered trade mark of Oxford University Press
in the UK and in certain other countries

British Library Cataloguing in Publication Data
Data available

ISBN-13: 978-0-19-919982-2
ISBN-10: 0-19-919982-5

1 3 5 7 9 10 8 6 4 2

Available in packs
Stage 12 More Stories B Pack of 6:
ISBN-13: 978-0-19-919981-5; ISBN-10: 0-19-919981-7
Stage 12 More Stories B Class Pack:
ISBN-13: 978-0-19-919988-4; ISBN-10: 0-19-919988-4
Guided Reading Cards also available:
ISBN-13: 978-0-19-919990-7; ISBN-10: 0-19-919990-6

Cover artwork by Chris Smedley

Printed in China by Imago

Chapter One

Ever since I was small, it had just been Dad and me.

Mostly, I didn't miss having a dad and mum, because Dad did both jobs really well. He was handy with a vacuum cleaner and my Nan said he could iron for England.

But there was one thing he couldn't do, however hard he tried.

He made brilliant spaghetti. He made delicious pizza. He made an ace sausage casserole.

But he couldn't make cakes. Somehow they always came out flat, heavy and hard.

He tried disguising them under
layers of icing, but it was no good.

My friend Sonia would say, 'I'd love
to come for tea. Your dad's a really
good cook, but please don't make me
eat his cake.'

Then, my Nan broke her dentures on one of Dad's raspberry buns.

She had to go around for a whole week with no top teeth. After that I said, 'Please Dad, don't make cakes ever again. Go to the supermarket and buy them, just like everyone else.'

He promised he would. Phew, what a relief. Baking always made Dad so miserable. When he was miserable, I was too.

Chapter Two

Then, one morning in assembly Mrs Tuttle, our head teacher, stood up and said, 'Now children, I expect you know that our Christmas Fair is only a few weeks away.'

'Boring,' I whispered to Sonia. My eyes rolled upwards. My eyelashes fluttered. I yawned loudly.

Sonia giggled and Mrs Rose, our teacher, leaned across and hissed, 'Jacqueline Green and Sonia Small. If I have to tell you off once more, you'll both be kept in at lunchtime.'

'And this year,' Mrs Tuttle continued, 'Sid's Cycles have very kindly agreed to give us a bike as First Prize in the Family Decorate a Cake Competition.'

'Oh great,' I whispered to Sonia. Dad was pretty good at decorating cakes.

I badly wanted a new bike, but we couldn't afford one. At least that's what Dad said. Now, with a bit of luck and a lot of icing sugar, we could win one instead. Easy!

Then, only seconds later, my dream was shattered into hundreds of tiny pieces.

Mrs Tuttle said, 'But this year, just to make the competition a bit harder, we want you to make the Christmas cake as well. So tell your mums and dads to get baking!'

'Hard luck,' said Sonia, rather spitefully, I thought. 'Looks like it'll be me getting the new bike after all.'

I glared at her and sniffed. She was right though.

Sonia's mum made cakes that were so light they almost floated. There was no way Dad could beat Sonia's mum, was there? Anyway, he'd promised never to bake another cake. Ever.

Chapter Three

That evening I was clearing away the dishes after tea. Dad was washing up saucepans at the sink.

'That chicken curry was delicious,' I said.

'New recipe,' he said. 'From Mrs Patel. It was good, wasn't it?'

He started whistling. He looked happy.

'Curry must be really difficult to make,' I said. 'Much more difficult than cakes.'

'Mrs Patel says I learn fast,' he said – a bit smugly, I thought.

'Maybe,' I said carefully, 'you could learn to make cakes, if you practised. Hard.'

'HAH!' he said, so loudly that I jumped and dropped a plate on the floor. It bounced.

'That was lucky,' he said, and started to whistle again.

I picked up the plate.

Only there's this competition at school.

'What sort of competition?' Dad asked.

'First prize is a new bike from Sid's Cycles,' I said.

'Wow!' said Dad, impressed.

'What you have to do,' I said, 'is decorate a Christmas cake.'

'We could have a go at that,' he said, cheerfully. 'Do you remember that Christmas cake we saw in Lack's window once?

'It looked like a snow-covered mountain, with people skiing down it. There was even a little cable car.

'We could buy a cake and then we could decorate it like that ourselves.'

'But,' I said, waving a piece of paper under Dad's nose, 'you have to make the cake as well. It says so in the rules.'

'Now then,' said Dad firmly. 'No more cake-making. A promise is a promise and I'm not going to break mine.'

Chapter Four

Dad said the way I went on about the competition was like being dripped on by a leaky tap. It wore you down, bit by bit.

At first he said, 'No! No! No!'

Then, he said, 'I'll think about it.'

Finally, he said, 'Oh, all right, I'll try, but you'll have to help.'

'Of course I will,' I said.

But I couldn't make cakes either. What we needed was expert help and quickly. The competition was in two weeks.

I thought of Nan first, but she said, 'Not on your nellie.'

My nerves couldn't stand it!

Then, I asked Mrs Patel, but she said cheerfully, 'Oh, I can't make cakes either. They always come out flat, heavy and hard.'

Brilliant. We were just going to have to do it on our own.

Chapter Five

On Saturday morning, we went to the supermarket and bought:

We also bought a cake tin. Dad had thrown all our old ones away.

'My dad's going to win me a bike in a baking competition,' I told the girl at the check-out.

Dad gave a sickly smile.

As soon as we got home, I got out the recipe book Nan had found for us. It was called *Cake-making for Absolute Beginners*.

Dad set to work. He creamed the butter and sugar.

He beat the eggs.

He folded in the flour and fruit.

'There,' he said proudly, as he spooned the mixture into the cake tin.

He opened the oven door and
popped the cake in.

'The oven seems very hot,' I said, as
a blast of scorching heat nearly burned
off Dad's eyebrows.

'Nonsense,' he said.

Half an hour later, Dad looked miserably at the lump of charcoal he had just taken out of the oven. His head drooped.

'Never mind,' I said. 'We'll try again.'

Back at the supermarket, the girl at the check-out said, 'Making another cake? The first one must have been really good.'

Dad gave her a sickly smile.

This time we got the oven temperature just right. Dad popped the new cake into the oven and said: 'Phew. Time for a nice cup of tea.'

He turned to switch on the kettle.

'Dad,' I said, looking at something white in a bowl by the bread-bin. 'What's this?'

'Oh no!' he groaned. 'I've forgotten to put in the flour.'

By the time we made cake number three, we were both tired. But we took things slowly. We checked and double checked the oven temperature.

I ticked off the sugar, eggs, butter, flour and fruit. We put the timer on and when it went '*Ping*', Dad opened the oven door.

The cake looked brown, not burnt.
It hadn't sagged in the middle.

It smelled delicious.

When the cake had cooled down
a bit, Dad turned it out. Oh dear, the
fruit had sunk right down to the
bottom. It looked like a layer cake.

'Is it meant to do that?' asked Dad.

'No,' I said.

After that, Dad refused to try again. 'It's no good,' he said. 'I'm useless.'

'You're not useless,' I said. 'You just can't make cakes.'

You can do loads of other things.

But I might as well have been talking to a brick wall. He wasn't going to listen to a word I said.

Chapter Six

At school on Monday morning, Sonia told me all about her mum's cake.

'It's a sure thing,' she said. 'There's no way it isn't going to win first prize.'

I knew I couldn't bear to see Sonia riding that new bike, even if she was my best friend. I was going to have to do something, but I didn't know what.

The next day I was off school. I'd been sick in the night. Dad said it was my fault for eating so much of the layer cake.

Nan came over to look after me while Dad was at work.

I still felt a bit sick, so I lay on the settee and watched some daytime TV.

'Perhaps we'd better not watch this,' said Nan, when a cookery programme came on. 'It might make you feel worse.'

But when I saw that the programme was called *Desperate to Cook*, I sat up and started to watch.

'Hi everybody,' whooped Denzil
Doonut, top chef. 'How you cookin'?'

'We're cookin' fine,' screamed back
Denzil's adoring fans. They were
stamping their feet and waving
wooden spoons in the air.

'Goodness me,' said Nan. 'You'd
have to be daft to want to go on that
programme.'

I nodded, but when I heard what
Denzil said next, I changed my mind.

'It's Denzil's "Can't Make, Won't Bake" spot. All those terrible, useless, awful cooks out there: I want to see you on my show. No matter how bad you are, I promise you will not fail!! So write down this number and call in now. We're waiting to hear from you.'

It was Nan who made a note of the telephone number for me. But I wanted to make the call.

'Hello,' I said. 'I'm ringing about my dad. He needs help.'

'There's no one too desperate for Denzil,' the television people said.

'Good,' I said. 'How soon can my dad be on the show?'

At first Dad refused even to think about it.

'There is no way that I'm going on television,' he said. 'I'll make a fool of myself.'

'You won't,' I said. 'You'll have Denzil's expert help.'

But he wasn't going to budge.

It was Nan who came up with the answer.

'Look,' she explained. 'You ring the local paper and tell them your dad's going to be on Denzil's show. He'll have to do it then, or he'll look like a real scaredy cat, won't he?'

'Um,' I said. 'That's very naughty.'

'All in a good cause,' she said, dialling the number of the local paper and handing me the phone.

'Hello. You don't know me,' I told the reporter who took my call. 'But my dad's going to be on TV.'

'Well?' asked Nan, when I'd put the phone down.

'They'd like to interview him tonight,' I said.

When Dad came in from work and I told him what I'd done, he was hopping mad. He shouted at me. He even shouted at Nan.

'What a very sneaky thing to do,' he said crossly. 'And don't think you've won. I'll just tell them that you made a mistake and I'm not going to be on television after all.'

Then, the doorbell went. It was the reporter from the local paper. She had a photographer with her.

'You're wasting your time,' said Dad, 'because I'm not going on TV. I'd never get time off work. I'm much too busy.'

I looked at Nan in horror. Her plan wasn't going to work.

'That doesn't matter,' said the reporter. 'We'll run the story anyway.'

So they did, and the headline read:

DESPERATE LOCAL DAD 'TOO BUSY' TO GO ON TV COOK SHOW

'Well, that's it then,' I said to Nan. We were both looking at Dad's picture in the paper. 'He's not going to do the show and I'm not going to get a new bike.'

But Nan and I weren't the only ones looking at the paper. Dad's boss saw it too and he was on the phone to Dad, as quick as a flash.

'You'll be on that cookery show, or else,' he said.

'Great,' I said, 'I'm going to ring Sonia and tell her the good news. She'll be really jealous.'

Chapter Seven

So there we were, only two days later, in a real TV studio. Nan and I were sitting in the front row. Dad was up front under the lights. He was wearing an apron and a silly hat.

Denzil Doonut, star TV chef, was ready to help Dad bake the perfect cake.

'I've never, ever had a failure,' he said to his adoring fans. 'Not in the whole history of *Desperate to Cook*. I can turn even the most hopeless case into a top chef.'

I could see Dad was beginning to relax.

'How are you feeling?' asked Denzil.

'Great,' said Dad. 'With your help, I know I can do it this time.'

Denzil clapped Dad on the shoulder.

'That's my man,' he said. 'Now, are we ready to bake?'

'We're ready!' the audience shouted. Nan and I shouted the loudest.

Eat your heart out Sonia's mum,
I thought, *'cos my dad's going to win.*

At first, things went well. Dad measured out the butter and sugar. He tipped them into a big glass bowl and creamed them together with a wooden spoon.

Magic.

'Now add the eggs,' said Denzil.

Dad had six eggs to crack and he cracked them perfectly. The yolks and whites plopped neatly into the mixing bowl.

'Well done,' said Denzil. 'Now for the electric whisk to beat in those eggs.'

I think Denzil was about to say, 'And start off slow,' but he didn't get the chance. Dad had his mixer on full speed and was whisking fast. Butter, sugar and six raw eggs were whizzing round Dad's bowl.

'Turn it down!' Denzil was shouting. He was trying to smile at the same time, but he looked anxious.

But Dad couldn't hear him. The whisk was clattering round the bowl like a mad thing. Dad was losing control of his arm. Cake mix was flying in all directions.

Denzil was desperately trying to
grab the mixer off Dad, but it kept
slipping out of his hands.

Soon there was no cake mix in the
bowl. It was all over Dad and Denzil.

'Right. That's it. I've had enough
of you!' roared Denzil.

'Ooooh,' we all gasped.

'Aaaagh,' wailed Dad. He quickly dropped the mixer on the floor and backed away from Denzil.

Denzil stamped down hard on the mixer. *Crunch, bang, flash.* Then it burst into flames and set fire to his trousers.

'Don't panic!' said the producer, running on with a fire extinguisher. 'It's all under control.'

Panic? The audience were loving every minute. They thought it was part of the show.

Nan was laughing so much, tears were rolling down her cheeks.

But I didn't think it was funny.

In fact, I was so cross, I leapt on stage and tipped a whole load of flour and fruit over Dad's head.

He just sat there like he'd been caught in a snow storm.

As for Denzil, they had to carry him out of the studio. He wasn't shouting or crying or anything, but his whole body was rigid.

Nan said that he was in shock.

Dad started to giggle. Then he was laughing and laughing.

'He's hysterical,' said Nan. 'We'd better get him home fast.'

After he'd recovered, Denzil Doonut gave an interview in the national press.

He said he'd thought he could teach anyone to make a cake. He'd been proved wrong. He felt humble. He was going to dedicate his life to finding a Dad-proof cake recipe.

He said he'd never, ever met anyone as useless at baking as Dad.

'Well, that's something, isn't it?' I said later. Dad started laughing again.

Chapter Eight

Dad and I went along to see the judging of the Christmas Cake Competition, even though we hadn't entered a cake.

After all, Dad had done the very best he could. I couldn't ask for more, could I? I'd even made it up with Sonia. I'd said, 'I really hope you win,' and I'd almost meant it. She'd said, 'You can have my old bike if I do.'

The school hall was very full. All the cakes were laid out on a trestle table on the stage.

They were going to be judged by Dave Smith, Chief Editor of the local paper,

Mr Lack of Lack's Bakery

and Sid Stoat of Sid's Cycles.

They took their time. They looked at all the cakes carefully. They made notes on how nice they looked. Then the cakes were cut and they tried a slice from each one.

I could see Sonia's mum. She and Sonia had pushed to the front. They wanted to be right there when the winner was announced.

Finally, the judging was over.

'In third place,' said Mrs Tuttle, 'is the Hebblethwaite family. Well done. In second place are the Dixons with Mr Dixon's cake. Well done.

'But in first place ...' she paused.

Sonia's mum had her foot on the first step up to the stage.

'... is Sonia Small's mum. Well done, Mrs Small!'

'Oh, well,' I sighed. That was it. I slipped my hand into Dad's and squeezed it hard.

We were just about to go home when Mrs Tuttle said, very loudly, 'But before you all leave, we have some more prizes to give out. Is Jackie Green's father here?'

Dad looked surprised. He put up his hand. Everyone turned to look.

'Wonderful,' said Mrs Tuttle. 'Please come up here. Bring Jackie with you.'

The three judges took it in turn to shake Dad's hand and Sid Stoat clapped Dad hard on the back.

'I watched you on the TV,' he said. 'When Jackie tipped flour over your head, I laughed so much I was nearly sick.'

'Oh good,' said Dad.

'I think she should have a prize for that. That's why I'm going to give her a big bike too. As long as you mention my name the next time you're in the paper or on TV, that is.'

'Oh, I will, Mr Stoat,' Dad said.

Denzil Doonut had already called, pleading with Dad to try out another cake recipe, live on the show.

'And to help you with the baking over this Christmas, here is one of our special Christmas cakes,' said Mr Lack.

'And I'm going to give you a cookery spot in the paper,' said Dave Smith.

Everyone was clapping really loudly.

'Well done, Dad,' I said. 'Three prizes for NOT baking the best Christmas cake.'

Is there anything else you can't do?

About the author

One day my son, Nick, was off school, poorly. He lay on the settee, watching a TV cook show. It was for people who couldn't cook. It made me think about my husband, who cooks lots of fancy dishes, but hates making cakes. He made me a birthday cake one year, but left out the sugar!

I imagined him baking a cake for a school competition and getting in the most awful mess! Suddenly, I had an idea for a story where the dads win prizes, not the mums!